To
Winnie, Olive,
Rose and Nell

I hope you enjoy HTG.

Bobmst

X

To my boy, Alexander. Never stop chasing
your dreams, son. Biggest love always.

And to Jan White, who introduced me to
The Crescent City and was the inspiration
for this book.

-Lorraine Johnston
Glasgow, Scotland

Later Tartan Gator: A New Orleans Tale

© 2013 by Lorraine Johnston

PRT0313A

Library of Congress Control Number: 2013931895

Printed in the United States

ISBN-13: 9781620861967
ISBN-10: 1620861968

www.mascotbooks.com

LATER TARTAN GATOR

A New Orleans Tale

Lorraine Johnston

Illustrated by
Preston Asevedo

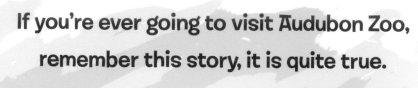

If you're ever going to visit Audubon Zoo,
remember this story, it is quite true.

The sign reads:

Do Not
Feed the Animals
at Any Time

There is an old alligator who sits in his pen.

He's got quite a story, it all started when...

Alligator loves when people stop by
to talk to him, stay a while, and then say goodbye.

And although he's quite a serious-looking alligator,
he smiles when people call to him, "Later, Gator!"

Some people were passing and ignored the sign:

"DO NOT FEED THE ANIMALS AT ANY TIME!"

They fed him some haggis; they were Scottish, you see.

But what they did was *very* wrong, if you ask me!

Do Not
Feed the Animals
at Any Time

4

Gator enjoyed the haggis very much indeed!

He wished for some more of the yummy, spicy feed.

Belly full and happy, he went for a little snooze.

But when he woke up, he was in for the blues!

He couldn't quite believe what his eyes were seeing.

As he looked down at his feet, it was *quite* disagreeing!

At first, he thought that it was just a *very* bad dream.

But it wasn't, it was real and it nearly made him scream!

Looking down, it was plain to see his two tartan feet
of green, gold, and purple; it was *really* quite neat.
He was no longer his usual alligator dark green.
He slumped away, too embarrassed to be seen.

"Later, Tartan Gator!" a little girl called.

Gator looked around; he was *completely* appalled.

"Why you looking so sad today?" she kindly asked.

"I'm Tartan!" he shrieked. "I don't know if it will last!"

"How'd that happen?" she asked, completely confused.

"The Scots fed me haggis! I'm *really* not amused!"

"Later, Tartan Gator," she said as she ran.

"I'll be back shortly; I have a great plan!"

She headed to the gates of Audubon Zoo.

She had an idea and knew *just* what to do...

Although it was quite a distance to this *very* special shop,
she headed for Magazine Street; she didn't even stop.
She got to Blue Frog Chocolates and quickly explained
what the problem was and how Gator had complained!

The owners of the chocolate shop were called Ann and Rick,

who were nice and kind to offer a solution pretty quick.

Into a box they put four Blue Chocolate Frogs for Gator.

The little girl said, "Thank you! I'll catch up with you later."

Gator started to wonder where the little girl had gone.

He worried a Tartan Gator wouldn't be welcome at Audubon.

As he was just about to give up all hope,
he heard the little girl run down the slope.

"Hey there, Tartan Gator. Look what I've got for you!"

Gator looked inside to see four chocolate frogs of blue.

"But little girl, didn't you read the sign? It's what got me in this mess."

"I know you shouldn't break the rules but do you *want* your Tartan-ness?"

Gator considered the very strange situation he was in.

The more he thought it over, the more his head was in a spin.

He wasn't *meant* to eat any food that visitors poked through.

And what if he ate all the frogs, and then he turned blue?

Tartan Gator decided to break the rules *just* one last time.
He had learned his lesson and would NOT repeat this crime.

He ate the Blue Chocolate Frogs one by one and gave a sigh.

He closed his eyes to have a snooze and tried hard not to cry.

The little girl said, "Later, Tartan Gator," and headed out the park.

She had done her good deed for today; it was nearly getting dark.

21

Do Not
Feed the Animals
at Any Time

Gator dreamt of pleasant things and *especially* being green!

Even during Mardi Gras, a Tartan Gator would not be seen!

Before long, the noisy birds woke him and he opened both his eyes.

There, down beneath his nose, was the most wonderful surprise.

One left green foot and one right green foot, too.

He promised **NEVER EVER** to eat food from visitors at the zoo!

Isn't reading FUN?

Here are two bookmarks for you

to cut out and use while enjoying

your favorite books, including

Do Not
Feed the Animals
at Any Time

LATER
TARTAN
GATOR

**This bookmark
belongs to**

_____

Do Not
Feed the Animals
at Any Time

LATER
TARTAN
GATOR

**This bookmark
belongs to**

_____

www.LaterTartanGator.com

Photographer - Ian Mortimer

Lorraine Johnston is from Glasgow, Scotland. She was a children's nanny for thirteen years and spent many hours making up stories for them using her vivid imagination. This was always met with giggles and laughter.

She worked for a New Orleans family, and through them, was introduced to The Crescent City. After many years and many visits, she considers New Orleans to be her home away from home.

Lorraine started writing in October 2011 and quickly discovered how much she enjoyed creating children's stories. She was passionate about writing a book set in New Orleans, while adding a little Scottish flavor to her story. *Later Tartan Gator* is her first children's book, but it certainly won't be her last!